M·K· BROWN

Crown Publishers, Inc.   New York

For Kalia

Manufactured in Japan

Library of Congress Cataloging-in-Publication Data. Brown, M.K. (Mary K.) Let's go swimming with Mr. Sillypants. Summary: Mr. Sillypants worries so much about his swimming lesson that he has a dream in which he turns into a fish. [1. Swimming – Fiction. 2. Humorous stories] I. Title. PZ7.B81616Le 1986   [E]   85-29900 ISBN 0-517-56185-9
10 9 8 7 6 5 4 3 2 1 First Edition

Very special thanks to Mr. Brian McConnachie.

Here comes Mr. Sillypants.
He has just signed up for swimming lessons.

What if all the other people in the class are better than I am?

I think I'll have a sandwich. Let's see . . . tomatoes, lettuce, olives, cheese,

pickles, tuna, peanut butter, mayonnaise, salami, cheese, pickles, olives, lettuce, and mustard.

A perfect sandwich.

What a nice dream!
I must be on the desert.
The sand is really hot on my feet
and I'm **very** thirsty.

Something tells me
to go this way.

And it was.